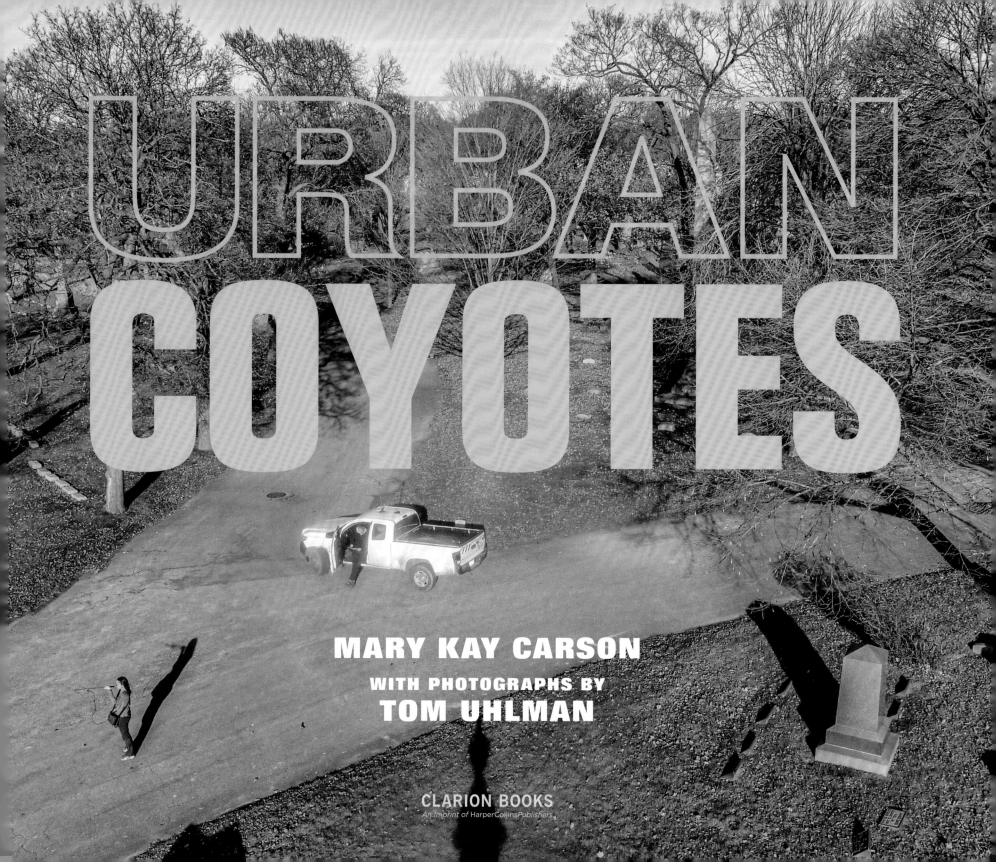

URBAN COYOTES

MARY KAY CARSON

WITH PHOTOGRAPHS BY
TOM UHLMAN

CLARION BOOKS
An Imprint of HarperCollinsPublishers

Clarion Books is an imprint of HarperCollins Publishers.

Text copyright © 2024 by Mary Kay Carson

Photographs copyright © 2024 by Tom Uhlman

Aerial maps pp. 46–47 courtesy of Urban Coyote
Research Project
Shutterstock/no_frames, pp. 11, 66
Shutterstock/mamita, p. 18
Shutterstock/DenysHolovatiuk, p. 31

Library of Congress Control Number: 2023944480
ISBN 978-0-06-327147-0

Typography by Michelle Bigman
24 25 26 27 28 RTLO 10 9 8 7 6 5 4 3 2 1

CONTENTS

CHAPTER ONE

THE GRAVEYARD SHIFT

"She's here somewhere," says a dark-haired woman holding up an antenna.

Cara Ratterman walks carefully around tall tombstones and flat grave markers. Her steps crunch the low, not-yet-green grass. The chilly March air carries a bite of wind. Bare trees rattle their branches. Rosehill Cemetery doesn't have many visitors today. At least, not human ones.

Cara stops. She listens. *Beep . . . beep . . . beep . . .*

Listening takes concentration in the middle of Chicago. Cars honk, trucks growl, buses rumble. An endless stream of vehicles circle the streets surrounding the cemetery. Airplanes soar and helicopters thwap overhead. Grown-ups yell and kids shout. Machines that fix streets, heat buildings, and load trucks thump, squawk, and roar. Big cities are noisy places.

◄ Cara searches for a collared coyote in a Chicago cemetery.

◄ Cara uses an antenna to find a collared coyote.

► Cara listens to the receiver in the shoulder bag while moving the antenna.

▲ The receiver makes beeping sounds when a collared coyote is nearby.

Beep . . . beep . . . beep . . . The soft sound comes from an electronic device. Cara carries the beeping toaster-size receiver in a shoulder bag. The receiver has knobs and switches like an old-fashioned radio. A dangling cord connects it to the antenna. She holds up the antenna with her right hand while fiddling with the receiver's control knobs with her left.

And she listens. *Beep . . . beep . . . beep . . .* The beeping sound means the receiver detects a signal. It's coming from a transmitter. The closer the transmitter, the stronger the beeping signal.

It's like playing a game of Hot or Cold. Loud beeping means the transmitter is nearby. *Hot!* Soft beeping means it's far away. *Cold!* To track down the transmitter, Cara moves in the direction that strengthens the beeping. What if the beeping fades while she's standing still? That means the coyote is moving away.

IT'S LIKE PLAYING A GAME OF
HOT OR COLD

Yep, the beep-triggering transmitter is on a coyote. A living, breathing, furry, four-legged, toothy wild animal. The coyote wears the transmitter on a collar around its neck. *Her* neck, actually.

Cara is seeking coyote number 1299, who is female. She's lived in Rosehill Cemetery with her mate for years. The pair have hunted prey, survived snowstorms, and successfully raised litters of pups among the headstones. During the past few months, coyote 1299 slept away many of her days in a culvert, a wide pipe that drains roads. A metal culvert isn't a typical winter hangout for a coyote. It's an unusual resting spot—even for city dwellers like her.

But that's the thing about coyotes. They don't necessarily do what's typical or usual or what's expected or predicted. Coyotes are rule breakers.

Beep . . . beep . . . beep . . . Cara starts walking again, back and forth under a granite-gray sky. Coyote 1299 isn't hunkered down in the culvert today. Her signal is coming from a different area of the cemetery. Cara crosses the same stretch of grass and graves once, twice, three times.

"Her signal is so strong here," Cara says, letting the antenna drop to her knees. Frustration shows on her face. It's like being unable to find something you know is there. A dropped earbud in the car. Homework in a book bag. It's maddening!

Ignoring the equipment for a moment, Cara stops and takes a good hard look around. A few feet away is a big catalpa tree. Last year's seedpods dangle from its still-bare branches. Where its trunk meets grass on one side, there's scattered sawdust and bits of bark. Above the scrapings is a dark hole, smaller than a paper plate.

"She's in the tree!" exclaims Cara with a big grin. And

▲ Cara discovers the tree where coyote 1299 is sleeping.

► It takes a sharp eye to spot coyote 1299 inside the hole.

COLLARED COYOTE 1299 PEERS OUT FROM HER TREE HOLE.

sure enough, two calm yellow eyes peer out of the dim. Curled up inside a hole at the tree's base, coyote 1299 awakens from a nap. The coyote was right here the entire time.

Only fifteen feet (4.6 meters) or so from the curb in a landscaped urban cemetery, the wild coyote hunkers down inside the catalpa tree. As coyote 1299 shifts in her den, she flashes a bit of the dirty tan collar encircling her neck. Then she blinks twice and goes back to sleep.

Mystery solved, Cara heads to a pickup truck with a large antenna sticking up out of its cab's roof. The metal antenna is oddly old-fashioned, like something you'd see strapped to the chimney of an abandoned house. Safety signs on the tailgate declare: Wildlife Survey Vehicle. Keep Alert for Sudden Stops and Turns.

Cara slides behind the wheel, grabs a clipboard off the passenger seat, and records coyote 1299's location, noting the tree den. Then it's time to move on. She's got other collared coyotes to find. And beastly Chicago traffic to battle. It's all in a day's work for urban-wildlife techs like Cara.

◀ The Urban Coyote Research Project vehicles stand out in Chicago traffic.

ONE OF THE PROJECT'S COLLARED COYOTES TRIES TO IGNORE CARA.

Stan has been studying Chicago's coyotes for nearly thirty years.

BIG-CITY COYOTES

This is the Urban Coyote Research Project. Its researchers study coyotes in Cook County, Illinois. The crowded county is home to more than five million people and includes the city of Chicago. Scientists have been studying the citified coyotes of Cook County for nearly twenty-five years.

Urban ecologist Stan Gehrt (pronounced "*gare*-it") started the project in the late 1990s. Back then he was a research biologist studying raccoons, deer, and skunks in the Chicago region—"Your standard urban wildlife," says Stan. "And then coyotes started showing up." In parks and backyards, on suburban streets and city sidewalks.

Wildlife agencies didn't know why it was happening. Neither did scientists. "Including me or any other biologists," remembers Stan. Suddenly seeing coyotes in their neighborhoods upset many residents. "People were not used to the idea of urban coyotes."

Coyote-spotting Chicagoans called 911. They flooded animal control agencies with coyote complaints. People feared the predators would bite kids, attack pets, and

▲ Chicago, Illinois, is the most populous city in the midwestern United States.

▶ The winter coat of a coyote is more than four inches (10 cm) thick.

spread diseases. Communities wanted the coyotes "removed," which meant killing them. Animal control agencies did try to get rid of them. "But they still kept showing up," says Stan. Urban coyotes weren't going away.

A Cook County wildlife official asked Stan to do a quick research study, just one year, to find out some basics: how many coyotes were out there and whether they were a danger to anyone. Stan expected to find just a few city coyotes. And he suspected most were visitors, perhaps young wanderers or lost loners who quickly moved on after dodging cars for a few days. "Nine million people live in the greater Chicago area," says Stan. "We didn't think very many coyotes could thrive in such a highly urbanized area." How long would it take to find out the truth?

"It took exactly one night," remembers Stan. "The very first night after we collared our first animal, I realized we were wrong about all of that." Cook County's coyotes had already dug in. Generations of pups were finding plenty to eat amid the city streets, parks, and green spaces.

Coyotes had chosen the Chicago city life—and they weren't going anywhere. Neither was the "quick" research study. The Urban Coyote Research Project continues to collar and track, study and learn about these supersurvivors nearly a quarter of a century later. "They're very, very complicated animals," says

COYOTES HAD CHOSEN THE CHICAGO CITY LIFE— AND THEY WEREN'T GOING ANYWHERE.

Stan. Armed with evolved instincts and extreme adaptability, coyotes thrive in all sorts of places, including downtown.

Discovering Chicago's coyote population kicked over a kettle of new questions—as scientific discoveries often do.

 WHERE did the coyotes come from—and why?

 ARE they a danger to Chicagoans?

 WHERE are Chicago's coyotes denning and raising pups?

 ARE they eating pets and garbage or rats and rabbits?

 DO wildlife officials need to manage urban wildlife?

 DO predators create healthier urban ecosystems?

Answering scientific questions like these requires scientifically collected information, or data. *Show me the data!* And that's what the Urban Coyote Research Project does. Researchers monitor coyotes, such as female cemetery citizen coyote 1299, for years. The project has collected data on Chicago's coyotes for over two decades and doesn't plan to stop anytime soon.

The project is research with a big mission: helping city-dwelling coyotes and humans live together in peace. And to prove to a suspicious public that prey-gobbling predators come with benefits. Coyotes eat disease-spreading vermin, and their biodiversity-boosting powers can transform urban green spaces into ecosystems that support more birds, butterflies, and other native wildlife.

After all, a single species now dominates all life on Earth. And as humans continue converting forests to factories and savannas to shopping malls, wildlife's future is uncertain. Can such a crowded world find space for wild animals, especially those predators that feed themselves using the toothy tools of their trade? Are coyotes outdated? Do they belong only in zoos and national parks? Or is there still space for the smart, curious, wild dog native to only the Americas?

Collecting tracking data can help scientists determine the challenges and benefits of coexisting with coyotes. But it takes work. Because before any collar goes on a coyote, it first must be caught.

Meet an
URBAN-WILDLIFE ECOLOGIST

When coyotes first trotted into Chicago, back in the 1990s, there weren't many city-wildlife scientists to call. "I was pretty much the only one doing that . . . at least in the Chicago region," says Stan Gehrt. Urban-wildlife ecologists like him were rare.

Growing up in the small town of Chanute, Kansas, Stan spent time outdoors searching for animals. "My challenge was to try and capture and bring home every single animal I possibly could," Stan says with a laugh. The Gehrt family tolerated most of his critters. But his mom did say no the time Stan showed up with a large aquatic rodent.

"I had been stalking this muskrat for days," remembers Stan. It lived in a not-so-nearby pond that Stan rode his bike to. "After trying and trying, I did actually catch the guy by the tail." But when he arrived home holding a muskrat, his mom wouldn't let him keep it in the bathtub as he'd planned. "I was crushed," says Stan. "I had to ride my bike all the way back and let the muskrat go."

Coyotes are native to Kansas where Stan grew up. "They were always around," he says. "I was always fascinated by them." One night while on a family camping trip, his dad suggested they try to call to coyotes by

◀ Coyote fur has "the perfect color combination to disappear in the background," says Stan.

▲ Coyotes are adaptable animals, able to survive in many kinds of habitats.

mimicking their yips and howls. "Lo and behold, the coyotes answered. It was a pretty eerie sound."

Years later, when Stan was a biology student in college, a gig tracking wolves in Canada set him on the path of wildlife researcher. "I liked it and decided that's what I wanted to do," remembers Stan. He became a wildlife ecologist, a scientist who studies wildlife relationships in ecosystems and the environment.

More scientists study urban wildlife these days. And there's more of it to study. City-dwelling predators, or urban carnivores, have become a worldwide phenomenon. Coyotes in Chicago are just one example. "Hyenas in Ethiopia are living in downtown areas," says Stan. "Leopards in India live in or around major metropolitan areas." Long-absent brown bears and wolves are showing up near European cities too. "It's an interesting time to be involved in this kind of research."

CHAPTER TWO
COLLARING CITY COYOTES

Aaarrkk, aaarrkk, aaarrk!

Loud barks echo inside a large equipment garage. Each string of sharp, short barks bounces off the concrete walls. Did someone bring her dog to work today? If so, it doesn't sound happy about being here.

Aaarrkk, aaarrkk, aaarrk!

A man walks toward the source of the high-pitched canine complaints and stops at what looks like a dog crate covered in draped towels. Shane McKenzie lifts the edge of a faded blue towel. Wary, wild animal eyes look out. The animal's coat is golden and thick, ears triangular, and snout pointy. A coyote! She's the mystery barker. Soon-to-be coyote number 1390.

"Let's get her started," Shane says softly. The coyote shakes nervously, her bony shoulders shivering. She's smaller under all that fur than he first suspected. Is she a teen coyote?

No one likes being caged, especially wild animals. It prevents both of their go-to instincts: flight *and* fight. Experienced wildlife scientists like Shane know the young coyote feels defenseless. *Get yourself captured* was not on her to-do list last night. Now she's caged, inside

▲ Cara and Shane unload a captured coyote from the truck.

▲ Cara and Shane carry in a captured coyote.

▲ A newly captured coyote nervously looks out from the cage.

COLLAR-WEARING COYOTES LIKE THIS ONE ARE THE BACKBONE OF THE URBAN COYOTE RESEARCH PROJECT.

a building, and surrounded by Carhartt-clad humans. Shane's team of pros moves in quickly and quietly, speaking in low soothing voices. No one wants to make it worse for her.

Shane smoothly slides a needle into the coyote's rump. The tranquilizing drug works quickly. Soon her head is nodding, then she's limp with deep sleep. Now the work begins.

Collar-wearing coyotes are the backbone of the Urban Coyote Research Project. Over the past twenty years, more than five hundred have been collared and tracked. Each captured coyote starts out like this one, going through a kind of registration process. And every sign-up session ends with a custom-fitted radio collar.

First up for sleeping beauty is a weight check. Two pairs of surgical-gloved urban-wildlife tech hands gently lift coyote 1390 out of the cage. They maneuver her into a net sling hanging from a scale.

"Eleven point seven," says Cara, reading the scale.

"Eleven point seven kilograms," repeats fellow urban-wildlife tech Blake Graber as he writes on a clipboard. That's not quite twenty-six pounds, the weight of a beagle, cocker spaniel, or other smallish dog. But the coyote looks bigger than that.

A clue as to why appears as Cara and Shane lay the coyote down on a big stainless-steel lab table. Their gloved fingers completely disappear into her fur. A coyote's winter coat is more than four inches (10 centimeters) long. Coyote 1390's puffy coat of fur makes her look bigger. Heavy fur traps body heat, shields skin from thorns and bites, and looks nice too.

▲ Project researchers gently weigh coyotes in a net sling.

▶ Shane and Cara get a tranquilized coyote ready for processing.

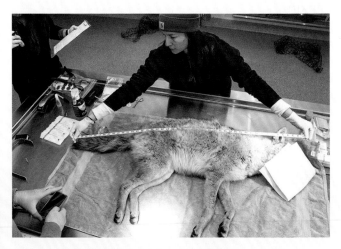

▲ Researcher Emily Zepeda measures a coyote's body length.

16

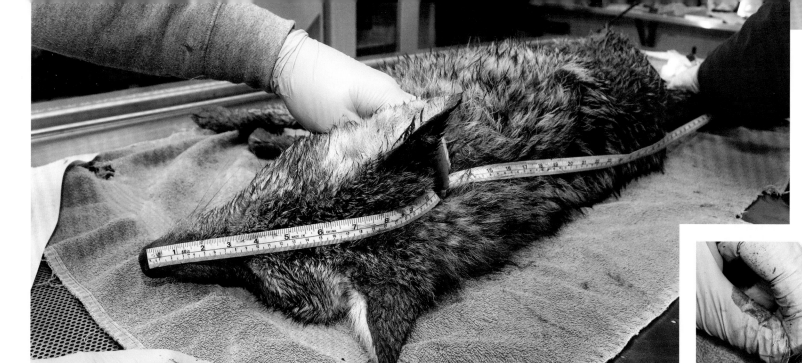

Cara leans over the coyote and squeezes some moisturizing drops into the animal's eyes. The knockout drug stops the eyes from blinking, so the drops help keep her eyes moist. A folded brown paper towel acts as an eyeshade. "The bright lights are drying," explains Cara.

With the coyote weighed and settled on the table, everyone works quickly to collect the coyote's information before she wakes up. Blake stretches a measuring tape down the coyote's body and records the length. Then he moves on to measuring and recording tail length, ear height, and paw size.

Size matters for predators like coyotes. The predator life isn't easy. Hunting, killing, and eating other animals takes a lot of energy. A predator's muscles and brain burn through stored calories as it looks for, chases, and attacks prey. What's an unsuccessful night of hunting called? A calorie deficit. It's like an Uber driver not collecting enough money from riders to pay for gas and keep going. The predator goes to sleep both hungry and with less gas left in the tank for tomorrow's hunt. Survival takes math.

▲ Ear height is sometimes measured after a coyote has gotten an ear tag.

There's pressure on predators to feed themselves without wasting energy. Larger prey size helps a predator's energy budget. They've evolved to focus on prey that's worth the work. That's how ecosystems support many predators. Not all hunters seek the same prey, and most predators prefer one prey to another.

This is true for members of the dog family, or canids. Wild dogs evolved to hunt size-suitable or size-specific prey. North America's own wild canids come in small, medium, and large—otherwise known as fox, coyote, and wolf.

Being the continent's big dog might *seem* great. But with an average weight of 50 kilograms (110 pounds), wolves need big food in order to thrive and feed a pack. Wolf packs target moose, elk, and bison for family-size meals.

Medium-size canids, including 11.7-kilogram coyote 1390, do not need a local elk herd to survive. Rodents and rabbits provide plenty of fuel for a country coyote. "Their favorite food is voles," says Stan, referring to the round, snackable, mouse-size rodents. "A coyote would probably get fat if it was eating nothing but voles its whole life, whereas wolves can't do that."

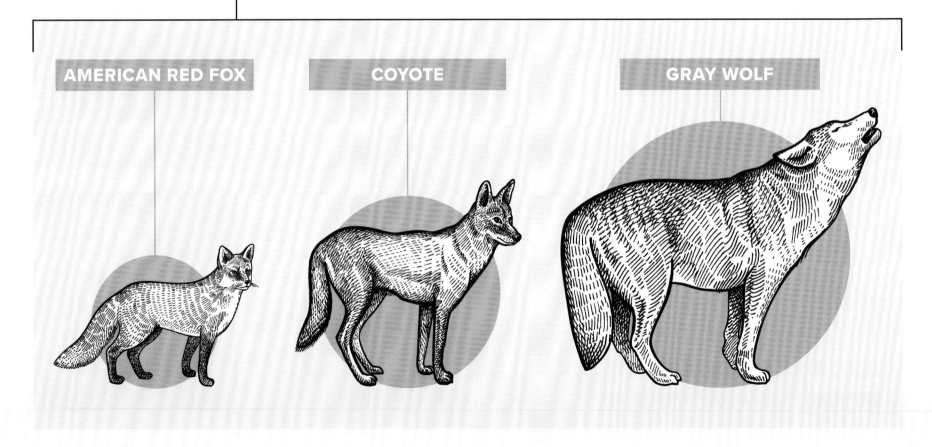

AMERICAN RED FOX

COYOTE

GRAY WOLF

What's in an
URBAN COYOTE'S MEAL KIT?

That's a crucial question for the Urban Coyote Research Project. Many people view coyotes as garbage-scrounging, dumpster-diving, pet-gobbling pests. Are Chicago's coyotes dining on trash and kitty cats?

▲ Coyotes help control deer populations by preying on fawns.

▲ Coyotes eat lots of Canada goose eggs in the Chicago region.

THE PREFERRED PREY OF COYOTES ARE RABBITS AND SMALL RODENTS LIKE CHIPMUNKS AND WOODCHUCKS.

▶ Coyote whiskers contain the animal's food history.

Results so far show that coyotes living in and around Chicago prefer natural foods for the most part. Rodents— voles, mice, rats—make up their main menu. They hunt rabbits and young deer—fawns—too. Urban coyotes also scavenge, snacking on carrion (dead animals), fruit, and bird eggs.

Back in the lab, Cara checks coyote 1390's eyes to make sure she's still unconscious. "She looks okay," says Cara to Blake. He nods as he snips away fur from a small spot of coyote 1390's leg. Meanwhile, Shane prepares a syringe. "Ready for the blood draw," says Blake.

Blood samples provide disease information. And that's a big deal. Wildlife diseases can become human diseases. The whole world learned that during the coronavirus pandemic. COVID-19 is one of many zoonotic pathogens—disease-causing germs that spread from animals to humans.

Rabies is another species-crossing virus, though Chicago has never seen a rabies-infected coyote. The blood tests look for Lyme disease, too, the infection spread by ticks.

Humans aren't the only ones at risk from coyote-carried germs. Coyotes can be infected with pathogens that harm pets, such as heartworm, the distemper virus, and parvovirus. Coyotes passing diseases to pets or people appears to be rare. But keeping track of disease levels in coyotes is a valuable tool for public health scientists, especially those on the lookout for the next epidemic.

Shane caps the blood vial and rubs a bit of alcohol on coyote 1390's leg. "Her DNA will be decoded too," says Shane.

"This will help us find out," says Shane, holding a pair of little scissors. He snips a whisker off the snout of sleeping coyote 1390 and drops it into a small envelope. The whiskers hold a record of what the coyote has eaten. By analyzing the chemical signatures deposited in slow-growing whiskers, researchers get a picture of the animal's diet. This method is more high tech than studying the stomach contents of road-killed coyotes or sifting through scat (poop!) for bits of bone, fur, and burritos.

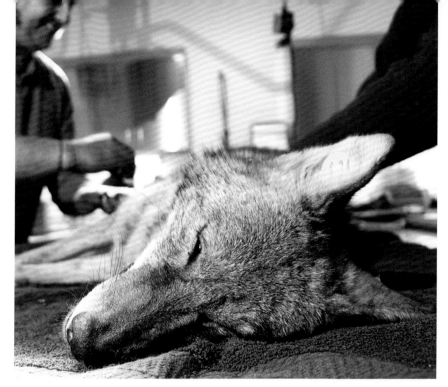

▲ Shane prepares a sedated coyote for its blood draw. Processing and collaring coyotes would be impossible without tranquilizing them.

▲ Cara carefully takes a blood sample from a sedated coyote.

That's right, the project has built a genetic family tree of all the coyotes in the study.

Cara picks up a red plastic rectangular device and waves it over coyote 1390's shoulder blades, scanning for a microchip. Veterinarians often implant these rice-grain-size identification chips under the skin of dogs and cats to help owners find lost pets. Wildlife scientists also use microchip tags to study recaptured animals over time. If an animal is already microchipped, the handheld scanner will pick up the tag, beep, and display an identification number.

"Nope," says Cara, setting the scanner down. No beep, no tag. That means the project didn't microchip coyote 1390 as a pup. Every spring, Shane's crew finds coyote dens and implants microchip tags in the pups. Usually, the found pups belong to a collared coyote the team's been tracking. (More pupping excitement later on!) Because coyote 1390 isn't chipped, her

THE PROJECT HAS BUILT A FAMILY TREE OF ALL THE COYOTES IN THE STUDY.

parents are likely uncollared. Not every den of pups gets found and microchipped. Perhaps she moved into the area recently. Her DNA will clue the project in on her heritage.

Coyote 1390's nails provide hints about her regular haunts and hunting grounds. Shane holds a limp paw and runs his thumb along the tips of her dark nails. They're a little worn down, but not a whole lot. Coyotes who spend all night trotting on concrete or asphalt wear down their nails more than those running around on dirt or grass.

The project collars coyotes living all over Cook County. Some coyotes live in suburban areas or in the county's system of forest preserves. Others live nearer the city center, finding food and shelter in green spaces along train lines and in cemeteries. Coyote 1390 came from an urban area that has a walking path and green space nearby. Her nails back that up. "Midway between city and forest preserve," says Shane.

Shane is a bit of a Chicago coyote whisperer. He's worked on the Urban Coyote Research Project for nearly a decade. Shane's captured and collared so many coyotes that at this point, he can tell a lot about each animal, including its age, just by looking at it.

Shane gently pulls back coyote 1390's lips to get a better view of her teeth. They look nice—white and sharp. "Not

◄ Examining how worn down a coyote's nails are tells researchers where the animal has been living.

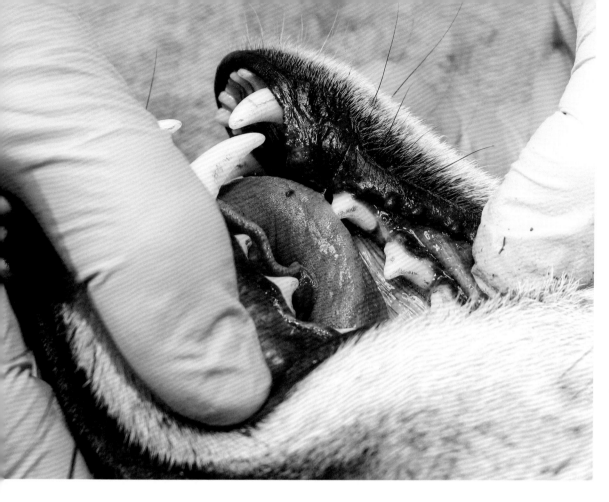

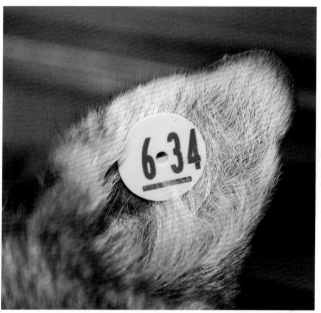

A coyote's teeth provide clues about its age.

▲ Female coyotes get yellow ear tags. Red tags are for males.

much wear," notes Shane as Blake snaps some photos of her chompers. "The more the molars look like rugged mountains, the younger the animal," Shane explains.

For female coyotes like this one, teats as well as teeth show age. The nipples on coyote 1390's chest, her teats, are hard to find under all the fur. A female who'd fed a litter of suckling pups would have more obvious teats.

"Not a mom," comments Shane. Based on that, her sparkling sharp teeth, and her slimness, Shane declares coyote 1390 a subadult. "That's an animal between one and two years of age and not yet breeding," he says. A teen coyote, in other words.

With all her information collected, it's time for our teen coyote to get some bling. Blake slides an ear into what looks like an industrial hole punch. When he pulls the tool away, a bright yellow ear tag remains. "Yellow is for girls and red for boys," he says with a smile while tagging the other ear.

Last up is the collar. It's light buff leather with a squarish battery box. Attached to one side is an antenna the width of a shoelace. Cara slips the collar around coyote 1390's neck like a belt. Meanwhile, Blake checks the collar's transmitter frequency with the receiver unit. This is coyote 1390's unique VHF signal. Project researchers will use it to find her from now

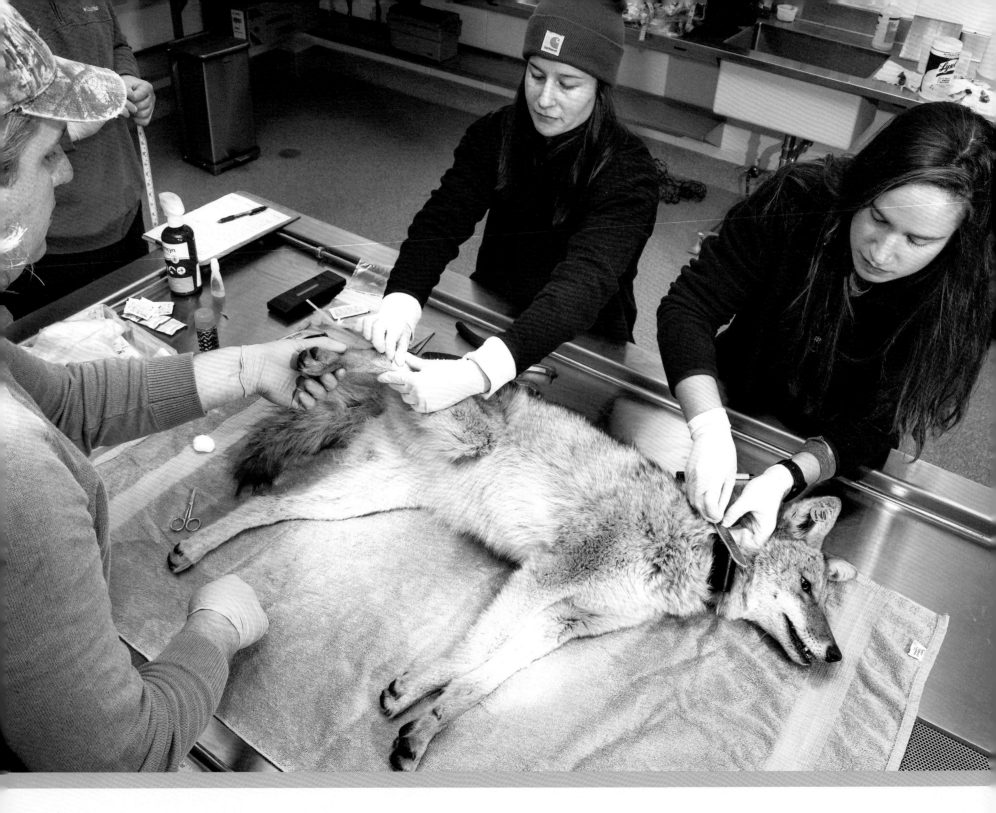

EVERYONE IN THE LAB WORKS SIMULTANEOUSLY ON A CAPTURED COYOTE TO PROCESS THE ANIMAL AS QUICKLY AS POSSIBLE.

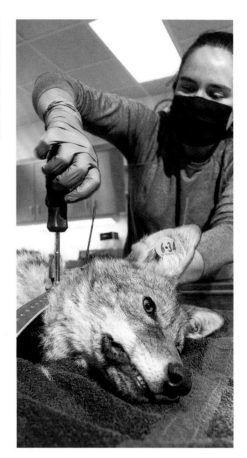

◄ Shane checks the collar fit around the tranquilized coyote's neck. It needs to be snug, but not too tight.

► Cara tightens the nuts on the transmitter collar while the coyote remains sedated.

on. Her collar transmits on a specific frequency, so it will serve as her identification signal whether she's seen or not. That's how Cara knew the coyote in the cemetery was nearby before finally spotting it inside the tree.

Cara takes care to fit the collar correctly and comfortably. Too loose and the coyote might wiggle out of it. But like all teenage subadults, coyote 1390 still has growing to do, so the collar can't be too snug either. Cara wedges two fingers under the collar to check for

room. "Not too tight," she says, running a hand down the young coyote's golden-furred back.

"And she's good," says Shane, helping to carry her over to the cage and set her gently inside. Coyote 1390 looks peacefully asleep as Blake covers the cage with towels. She'll wake up soon and not be happy to find herself still caged. But a quiet darkened space should soothe her nerves until she's set free later in the day. Coyote 1390 will be back on the hunt by nightfall.

▲ Coyote 1390 takes in the familiar smells while slinking out of the cage.

CHAPTER THREE

MESOPREDATOR MAGIC

Shane McKenzie's truck splashes over rain-filled potholes and wet pavement. Chicago winters tear up streets, but the driveways around the old hospital annex appear extra-overdue for road repair.

If the bumpy ride irritates coyote 1390, she doesn't show it. The newly collared coyote leans against the rear of the

cage. Airliners roar overhead, flying to and from nearby O'Hare airport. Does coyote 1390 recognize the sound? Do the scents drifting into the truck smell like home?

Shane stops the truck, walks around to the back, and opens the tailgate. The coyote sedative wore off hours ago, and coyote 1390 is now fully alert—and *on* full alert. The new

▲ And she's gone in seconds.

▲ With home in sight, coyote 1390 bolts for the bushes.

collar indents a ring into the fur around her neck. Her yellow eyes take in every movement made by the two-legged creature scooting the cage that holds her. She intends to be ready for whatever happens next.

The late-afternoon drizzle seems to be on break. Shane lifts the cage off the lowered truck gate and carries it a few yards before setting it down. Then he quietly slides the cage door open. Shane smoothly and quickly steps away, out of her path of escape. It's time for coyote 1390 to return home.

Coyote 1390 pokes out her snout, then her lowered head, sniffing furiously. In the next instant, her golden front paws hit the pavement and she springs free of the cage. She lopes

COYOTE 1390 IS NOW FULLY ALERT—AND *ON* FULL ALERT.

toward a section of flooded pavement at full speed. With three lightning-fast strides, she crosses the deep puddle, kicking greige water high into the air behind her. A yellow tag flashes from the back of each swiveling triangular ear. Then coyote 1390 leaps up and over a gravel mound—and disappears without looking back. Good luck, girl!

Beyond the gravel hill she just climbed lies a green space thick with tall, ouchy, spiky-topped weeds and tasty small prey. The young female coyote was captured here last night.

The cage sits empty under the shabby canopy of an old gas pump. It's sheltered from the returning sprinkles of rain. Construction debris, gravel, asphalt, and heaped-up pavement chunks surround the concrete strip that coyote 1390 just sprinted across. Her home turf looks more like a post-apocalyptic movie set than a wildlife habitat. But it's likely she and other pups were born and raised in this landscape of weedy brush and piles of junk.

AMERICAN SUCCESS STORY

Why does coyote 1390 live here? How did thousands (thousands!) of coyotes end up living in and around the third-largest city in the United States? That's what Stan Gehrt is working to figure out. "It's an amazing North American story that we don't completely understand," he says.

WESTERN NORTH AMERICA'S DESERTS HAVE BEEN COYOTE HABITAT FOR THOUSANDS OF YEARS.

◄ Coyotes have been in North America for more than a million years.

▼ Sagebrush scrublands have long been coyote territory.

▲ Coyotes were historically open-country animals, hunting in the prairies and deserts of western North America.

The beginning of the urban coyote's story is clearer. Coyotes historically roamed the big-sky prairies and deserts of western North America. They evolved as predators in wide-open spaces. The thick forests that once blanketed the eastern half of the continent belonged to wolves, bears, cougars, and other woodland predators.

Then European colonization happened. Colonists cleared forests to create farms and pastures. Felled trees fueled steamboats and trains, supplied lumber mills, and built boomtowns. Roughly half of the eastern United States was deforested by 1900. That created more open space.

While plowing farmland, creating pastures for livestock, and building towns, colonists killed predators. They viewed bears, cougars, wolves, and other toothy hunters as problematic pests. The government ran so-called predator-control programs

COYOTES EVOLVED AS PREDATORS IN WIDE-OPEN SPACES.

that paid bounty hunters per shot, trapped, or poisoned dead animal. Wolves howling became an unheard sound in nearly the entire United States. And coyotes lost their large canid competition.

Predator control targeted coyotes too. People tried exterminating them in all sorts of ways, says Stan. "Poisons, steel traps, guns, airplanes, dogs, fire . . . " he says. "And we don't have any impact on them at all." Wary, wily coyotes survived. They learned to avoid traps and poisoned carcasses, hide from hunters and dogs, and find new places to live.

Coyote culling continues today. Around a half a million die at the hands of humans each year in the United States alone. That's more than a thousand a day, every day. There are few restrictions on hunting and trapping coyotes in most states. In fact, contests offer cash and prizes for the biggest or most animals killed. The Humane Society of the United States considers wildlife-killing contests a cruel "blood sport," akin to dogfighting and cockfighting (both of which are illegal).

Being viewed as better-off-dead pests hasn't stopped coyotes from spreading. Removing wolves and forests opened the continent to coyotes. "In the last fifty to sixty years, they expanded their range to the eastern part of the United States and eastern parts of Canada, as well as to the north, all the way up to the Arctic Circle," explains Stan. Coyotes live in every state except Hawaii. "And now they've just recently crossed the Panama Canal." South America, here they come.

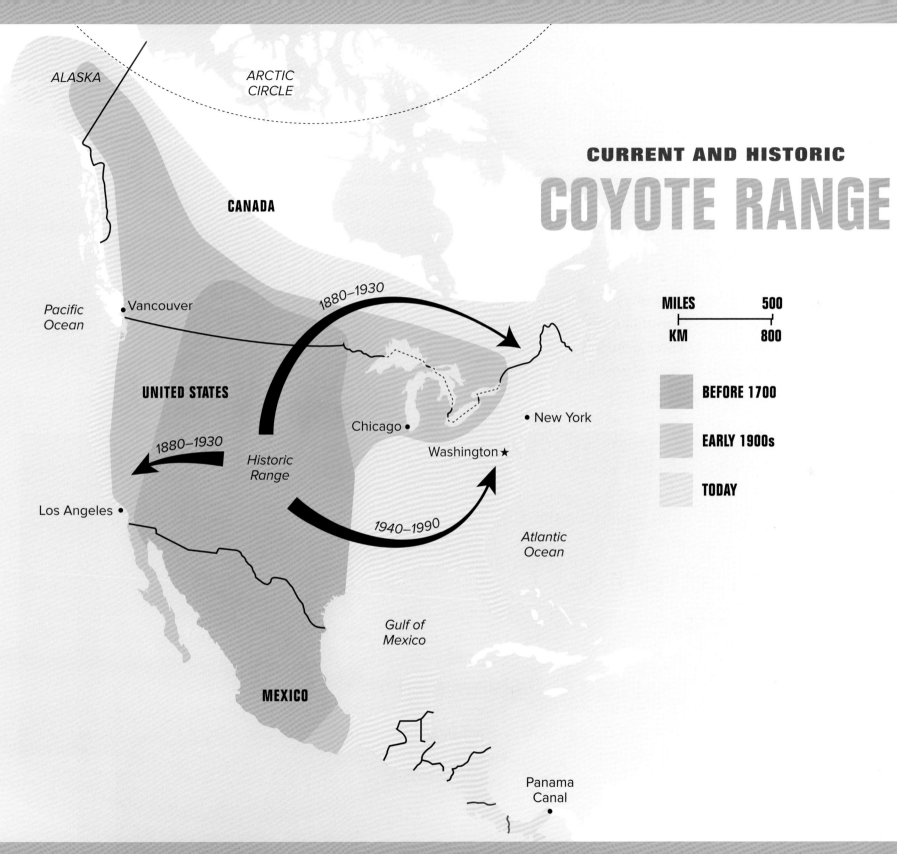

CURRENT AND HISTORIC
COYOTE RANGE

ALASKA

ARCTIC CIRCLE

CANADA

Pacific Ocean

• Vancouver

1880–1930

UNITED STATES

1880–1930

Historic Range

• Chicago

Washington ★

• New York

1940–1990

Los Angeles •

Atlantic Ocean

Gulf of Mexico

MEXICO

Panama Canal

MILES	500
KM	800

BEFORE 1700

EARLY 1900s

TODAY

RISE OF THE URBAN MESOPREDATOR

Ah, the 1990s. The Soviet Union broke up, grunge music went big, and the internet appeared. Coyotes, too, had a big end-of-the-century decade.

In the early 1990s, coyote fur became really cheap as wearing fur fell out of fashion. Many fur trappers called it quits on coyotes; there was just not enough money in it. "That crash in pelt prices dramatically affected the amount of animals that were harvested for their fur," explains Stan.

The boost in coyote numbers created "bumper crops" of young coyotes across rural America, all of them in need of new territories. They went searching farther and farther away from their wilderness and farmland birthplaces. Some of the young coyotes found space up for grabs in the outer semirural suburbs of metropolitan areas. Once those places got coyote-crowded, newer generations moved into proper suburbs, then eventually pushed into cities. The urban coyote was born.

Cities like Chicago were coyote-free environments for animals looking to establish new territories. Sounds sensible for coyotes to go there, right? But it's not something all predators will do. Why are coyotes easily able to make a new life in a place so completely different from where they were born?

◀ Coyote pups grow up fast.

▶ A hollow tree in a backyard makes a perfect place for coyotes to keep their pups.

▽ Cara watches coyote pups inside an old cistern den with help from an endoscope.

◀ A coyote pup sleeps in a neighborhood tree.

Coyotes are adaptable animals, able to survive in many kinds of habitats.

What's
IN A NAME?

The coyote's scientific Latin name, *Canis latrans*, translates to "barking dog." *Latrans* is the barking part and the genus name, *Canis*, means "dog." Other canid, or canine, family members in the genus include wolves (*Canis lupus*) and golden jackals (*Canis aureus*), as well as terriers, beagles, poodles, and other domestic dogs (*Canis familiaris* or *Canis lupus familiaris*).

Like many animals that live over an expansive area, coyotes come in a number of variations, or subspecies (Mexican coyotes, mountain coyotes, etc.). Each variation has its unique mix of traits. Two major variations are western coyotes and eastern coyotes.

▼ "Most people are surprised by how much color they have in their coat when viewed up close," says Stan.

Traces of wolf DNA is the eastern coyote's claim to fame. A bit of wolf heritage boosts their body size some. The historic wolf-coyote mixing probably happened around the Great Lakes a century or so ago, after people killed most of the region's wolves. Western coyotes moved in, and some leftover wolves interbred with those arriving coyotes, creating a somewhat bigger eastern coyote subspecies.

Some call the eastern coyote the *coywolf*. But since the mix is far from half and half, it's not a very accurate name. Most scientists call them eastern coyotes, not coywolves.

Another name thrown around is *coydog*, a mix of domestic dog and coyote. Coyotes and dogs rarely mate in the wild. Coyotes see dogs as threats or nuisances, not potential mates. Coyote parents raise pups as a team. This isn't true for domestic dogs, so the two species aren't well matched behaviorally either. People do create coydogs through captive breeding. It's often an attempt to breed a domestic dog with coyote characteristics.

HOW DO YOU SAY *COYOTE*?

The word coyote comes from the Aztecs. The indigenous people of northern Mexico called the animal *coyōtl* ("koh-*yo*-til"). Spanish colonists in North America changed the name to *coyote* ("koh-*yo*-tay"), its current Spanish pronunciation.

When English-speaking colonists moved into coyote territory, some adopted the Spanish name for *Canis latrans*. Others called them *prairie wolves* or *brush wolves*, names that faded over time.

While nearly everyone calls *Canis latrans* coyote today, its English pronunciation varies by region. Many people say "kie-*oh*-tee," copying the three-syllable pattern of the Spanish word. Others, especially Midwesterners, pronounce it "*kie*-yoat," with only two syllables. Both are correct, so no judgment!

▶ Cara tries to pick up a coyote collar's transmitter signal using a handheld antenna.

CHAPTER FOUR

TRACKING TRICKSTERS

Wildlife techs spend a lot of time sitting at red lights. At least, those working on the Urban Coyote Research Project do. Chicago's gridlocked traffic is as famous as its deep-dish pizza. (Yum!) The brake lights on Cara Ratterman's truck barely dim as she squeaks through a clogged intersection.

The odd-looking antenna jutting from the truck cab's roof swivels slowly. Then it stops. A few seconds later, the spindly metal contraption starts swiveling the opposite way. And then stops with a wobble. Can an antenna look frustrated? This one does. Or maybe it's the person controlling it. After more than an hour of searching, Cara has yet to find her four-legged target. "This is very unusual," she says.

The receiver remains stubbornly silent on the passenger seat beside Cara. Not a single beep. She keeps driving, again looping around the block, past the crowded Costco and busy sausage stand. She lifts her right hand to the cab's ceiling and grabs a white, dimpled knob—a golf ball. A metal rod pierces

▲ Blake checks the receiver for signals inside the truck.

the golf ball and acts as a lever. Moving it turns the antenna on the roof.

Driving around with an antenna made of thin metal rods attached to a tall pole can be challenging. "They get bent up easily," says Cara. Techs must watch out for low branches,

39

check the height marked on bridges and tunnels, and think twice before pulling into a burger drive-through.

Right now, Cara concentrates on listening while driving. The receiver refuses to beep. Coyote number 1386 should be here somewhere. Cara has been zeroing in on his morning location for nearly ninety minutes. "The idea is to circle around that point," she says. He can't have gone that far in the past couple of hours, can he? Most coyotes spend mornings sleeping off the night's hunt.

Most, but not all. Coyotes, especially urban ones, make their own rules, and coyote 1386 has no family or mate to anchor him. He's a solitary, or transient, male. That makes his movements extra-hard to predict.

Coyotes live in an organized social system of packs. The packs make up a grid of defended territories. Family members make up a coyote pack. "The nucleus of the pack is the alpha pair," explains Stan Gehrt. "Offspring of different ages make up the rest of the pack." A pack might include just parents and their new pups or a bunch of grown adult offspring too. Everyone in the pack is subordinate to the parents, or alpha pair. The alpha male and female run the show, and the entire pack defends its territory together.

▲ Chicago's downtown sits along the western shore of Lake Michigan.

◀ Chicago train yards feed railroad lines throughout the region.

▶ Notice the trees and corridors of green space along Chicago's extensive train lines.

Packless transient coyotes, such as coyote 1386, are often just traveling through an area. They're lone coyotes searching for available territory and the chance to start a pack of their own. Currently solo coyote 1386 seems to be looking for a place to settle down. Shane and crew trapped him at a nature center in Chicago's suburbs. Since his collaring, coyote 1386 has been drifting from place to place, perhaps hunting for a home territory to claim.

Over the past weekend, coyote 1386 traveled far from Chicago and then back, more than a hundred miles (160 km) round trip. "We've no idea why," admits Shane. The male coyote followed a river all the way up through Illinois and nearly crossed over the border into Wisconsin. After finding whatever he was looking for (or not), coyote 1386 turned around and came back. Now the well-traveled transient is traipsing about Chicago.

Cara hopes that tracking him down in the city might offer a clue about his weekend getaway. How did researchers know he almost went to Wisconsin? The collar around coyote 1386's neck includes a GPS tracker.

The Urban Coyote Research Project uses two kinds of collars. Simple VHF collars go on most coyotes. They're cheap and have

have to be big enough to wear them," Cara explains. As a full-grown male, coyote 1386 can handle a GPS collar. Satellites track the GPS-collared coyotes just like they track GPS-equipped cars and smartphones. But the coyotes' locations aren't available in real time. The programmed trackers send collected sets of logged locations for all the GPS-collared coyotes to a computer via satellite. It's coyote 1386's GPS location earlier today that Cara is using as a target. Without much luck.

Miles and miles of suburbs sprawl out from Chicago's downtown.

long-lasting batteries. (Ask a grandparent about VHF television.) Very high frequency, or VHF, transmitters on the collars send out VHF radio waves that the antennas pick up as beeping signals. "We have between forty to fifty with the VHF collars," says Stan. Fewer than ten of the project's coyotes wear collars supplemented with GPS trackers.

The Global Positioning System (GPS) collars are more expensive than the VHF collars—too pricey for the number of collars the project uses. (Science costs money, folks.) Nor do they last as long. Plus, GPS collars are heavier. "The coyotes

Cara's phone pings, a hopeful sound. Blake Graber, the other urban-wildlife tech, says he's picked up coyote 1386's signal nearby. Cara heads his way. The two techs rendezvous behind some large buildings. A fence runs along the wide alley, and beyond the fence are train tracks. Blake leans into Cara's truck, and the two chat as it begins to sprinkle. "It's gone now," says Blake of coyote 1386's signal. Has yet another wily coyote outsmarted humans?

Perhaps, but tracking VHF signals in the city is tough going, no matter who wears the transmitter. The VHF collars transmit radio waves by line of sight. That means if a coyote is on the other side of a building or hill, its signal is blocked. The searcher's antenna can't pick it up. Concrete, stone, and metals also refract (bounce) VHF radio waves. The beeping might sound like it's coming from one direction when it actually bounced there from elsewhere. "There's a learning curve to it, for sure," says Cara. All the interference in the city means that the truck antennas have half the range they'd have in suburban searches. In the city, the truck antennas can pick up signals only within a distance of a few football fields (300 to 500 meters).

Cara pulls on a rain jacket and leaves the truck. Not quite ready to give up, she plugs the handheld antenna into the receiver, slings it over a shoulder, shimmies through a gap in the fence, and climbs up the steep embankment to the train tracks. The landscape looks different from up there. Down to the right are the parked antenna trucks, a chain-link fence, and the backs of stores and businesses. Looking left, she sees a greener scene.

A series of small backyards line up below the left side of the tracks. Each patch of yard backs up to a high wooden fence. A hillside covered in weeds, shrubs, and small trees slopes down from the tracks to the wooden fences. Seen from up top, this strip of trackside green space goes endlessly off into the distance. An urban ecosystem of plants and creatures, including coyotes, live in this linear swath of habitat.

"He could be holed up along here," says Cara. She turns, repositions the antenna, and listens. Raindrops splash onto the antenna she holds up. *Plop, plop, plop.* Traffic roars nearby. Someone honks a horn. But there's not one beeping sound. Nothing.

Coyote 1386 might be long gone. "Coyotes can move quicker in the city," says Shane. "These railroad systems act like highways." Coyotes trot from one place to another along train tracks faster than cars can drive the same distance. "We can't keep up with them in the city," says Shane. "Versus in the suburbs, where we can usually get ahead of them."

Time for Cara and Blake to move on. Tomorrow is another day and another opportunity. And because coyote 1386's collar has GPS, Shane and the crew should get an automatic update on his position. They'll find the trickster transient soon enough.

HAS YET ANOTHER

WILY COYOTE

OUTSMARTED HUMANS?

SURVEY SAYS

The Urban Coyote Research Project tracks collared coyotes all year. The antenna trucks make rounds both day and night, collecting each collared coyote's position at least once a week. Blake and Cara trade off working nights and often drive a hundred or so miles (160 kilometers) a day.

The urban-wildlife techs help trap and collar coyotes too. The project limits trapping to late autumn and winter, when coyotes aren't caring for young pups. Shane says that capturing coyotes in the city center comes with extra challenges. "It can be difficult to find capture sites in Chicago," he says.

On the west and south sides of Chicago, there are some city blocks with more vacant lots than lived-in homes. The city tore down the houses on these sites decades ago. "Now that a lot's house is gone, is it a habitat for coyotes?" asks Shane. The project is trying to find out.

Not long ago, Shane thought he had one such weedy lot lined up as a capture site. "I was so excited about it," remembers Shane. But when he showed up, workers were

SHANE AND A GRADUATE STUDENT PRACTICE TRACKING COYOTES USING THE ANTENNA.

▲ A collared coyote.

steamrolling pavement and surrounding the site with fencing. The owner had decided to turn it into a parking lot. "It was grass a few months back, and now it's gone." Yet another problem to solve—something Shane actually enjoys about his job. "I'm always learning something new," he says.

The biologist has been with the Urban Coyote Research Project for more than a decade. Shane's trapped, collared, released, and tracked hundreds of coyotes in and around Chicago. He's also taught countless field techs and graduate students how to work with wild coyotes. "One of the reasons this project exists is to train people and give them experience working with wildlife," says Shane.

All the hard work studying collared coyotes in the Chicago area has paid off for science. One of the project's first findings is that many (many!) more coyotes are living in the city than anyone imagined. And most Chicagoans don't even realize the four-legged predators are around. That's a clear sign that "coyotes could live near people without necessarily coming into conflict with them," says Stan. And the project has data to prove it—unbiased data. "We weren't there to protect coyotes or promote them." Years of collared-coyote tracking has turned into decades of data, and patterns have appeared in the different environments Chicagoland coyotes inhabit—patterns indicating how coyotes establish their territories.

Coyotes defend their territories fiercely, running off or sometimes killing unwelcome coyote intruders. The need for territories is a hardwired, inflexible behavior. But while territories are must-haves, Chicago's coyotes appear able to establish and accept territories of different shapes and sizes. The exact makeup of a suitable territory depends on its location. Maps make the differences clear. Plotting all the location points of individual coyotes on maps reveals patterns. The territories of city-center coyotes and forest-preserve coyotes aren't the same. And the shape and size of a suburban coyote's territory isn't like a city-center or forest-preserve coyote's territory. Each of the three kinds takes advantage of available open space in a particular way.

The territories of coyotes living in forest preserves take up the most space. "A lot of the animals born in these forest preserves live their entire life there," explains Shane. Their nails are sharp because the coyotes rarely trot on concrete. Roads often serve as territory borders within the large preserves.

"And then there's the coyotes that live in what we call the

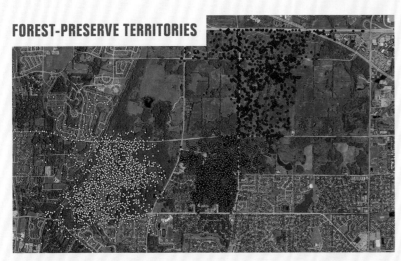

FOREST-PRESERVE TERRITORIES

▲ The yellow, blue, and red dots mark the logged locations of three different coyotes, each keeping to its own territory.

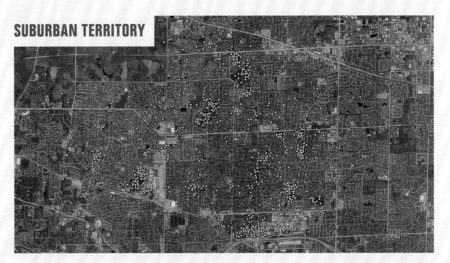

SUBURBAN TERRITORY

▲ The yellow dots mark the logged locations of a suburban coyote navigating a neighborhood grid.

matrix," says Shane. These suburbanites dwell in the grid of neighborhood streets, creating territories by connecting small marshes and other modest green spaces. Suburban or matrix coyotes are the animals most often seen by people, says Shane. "These are the ones cutting through your backyard and crossing your streets." Finding prey and defending a disconnected territory takes travel. Suburban coyotes are commuters, roaming between small patches of green space and marshland.

City-dwellers are a different kind of animal, says Shane. They act differently than both suburban and forest preserve coyotes. "Once they get to the city, these animals have adapted to understand that you live longer staying away from humans," he says. City coyotes build territories out of areas humans don't frequent, like train yards, abandoned lots, and the weedy edges along railroad tracks. They travel along unpopulated corridors beside trainlines, covering perhaps more distance but staying within a smaller overall area than other urban coyotes.

The mapped data from the project show that while the need for territories is hardwired, the shape and size of that territory is not. Coyote parents sometimes gift part of their territory to a grown pup, for example. And some coyotes live their entire lives in a single small cemetery. Chicago's coyotes are redefining what a territory looks like, carving out corners and pieces to call their own.

"Life must be good for the coyotes," says Stan. "There are still ways for them to increase, even within areas that have been occupied for many years."

CITY-CENTER TERRITORY

▲ The red dots mark the logged locations of a downtown-dwelling coyote along train lines and green space corridors.

CHICAGO'S COYOTES ARE REDEFINING WHAT A TERRITORY LOOKS LIKE, CARVING OUT CORNERS AND PIECES TO CALL THEIR OWN.

The loose dirt outside the hole under a root ball is a sign that a coyote den might be inside.

CHAPTER FIVE

FAMILY DOG LIFE

The first hot day of the year has sent Chicagoans into a frenzy. People mow lawns, grill food outside, and clean winter debris off patio furniture. Forget that it's only early May and most trees barely have leaves. The hot steamy air shouts *summer!*

Shane McKenzie and the crew cross the busy boulevard at a traffic light and walk to a small artificial lake. A big multistory retirement building rises from the lake's far side. Between here and there is a strip of green space—trees, bushes, blooming bluebells, and other wildflowers.

▼ A tuft of coyote fur is a sure sign.

▼ Coyote researchers go all in when investigating dens.

Shane points out the root ball of a huge fallen tree. Where the sprawling dead roots meet the ground, there's a pile of loose dirt. A closer look reveals bits of grayish fur on the lowest roots. It's a coyote den.

"No pups," says Shane. "It's the natal den." A flashlight beam confirms the hole's emptiness. Coyote number 1035 recently gave birth in this natal, or birthing, den. But the coyote parents already moved the pups. Coyotes transfer their pups when the youngsters outgrow a den space or if the site no longer feels safe.

This small neighborhood green space is coyote 1035's latest tracked position, so the new den should be nearby. The team members go into search mode, heading off in different directions, shining flashlights in holes and hollow trees, poking suspicious brush piles, and checking for doglike tracks.

Coyote pairs dig out dens or take over skunks', raccoons', or other critters' dens. Urban coyotes' dens sometimes show up in odd places—deep inside old cisterns or wells, under sheds, in crawl spaces under abandoned buildings. Finding dens isn't easy, thanks to coyote cautiousness.

"They try and pick the most secluded spot," explains Stan Gehrt. Being tied to a single spot like a den makes most coyotes uneasy. People mistakenly think coyotes live in dens all the time. They don't, says Stan. "Not unless they're sick, injured, or there's some other extreme event. They just go into dens to raise litters. And as soon as the pups are old enough, they get them out." Hanging out in the exact same place makes coyote pups vulnerable to predators—and makes parents nervous during denning time.

Stan finds the family life of coyotes endlessly fascinating. The behavior and biology behind coyote reproduction empowers the species' success and ever-growing expansion. How? The number of pups a mom births, litter sizes, and when young coyotes reach breeding age can change. It depends on the available food and open space that's around. And on how coyote-crowded their world is.

Let's start at the beginning. Coyote breeding happens in winter. "The peak is around Valentine's Day in Chicagoland,"

says Shane. (Cute, right?) One male and one female mate only with each other. The pair stay together for life. How do researchers know that for sure? The proof is in the pups.

Chicago coyote moms give birth in late April. "We go into the dens each year and microchip the pups," says Stan. (Remember scanning the captured coyote for a microchip tag on page 21?) "We also draw a little bit of blood and collect some hair." Scientists working with the Urban Coyote Research Project compare the pup DNA in those samples to

◄ This old cistern opening is plenty big enough for coyotes to get pups in and out.

▶ The spring bluebells might be nice, but they're not what Shane is looking for.

▲ Den searches start at the last known coordinates of a collared-coyote parent.

▼ Stan (left) is a master coyote-den finder, but volunteer help is welcome too.

their parents' genetic information. "We have yet to document a single divorce," says Stan. Coyote parents mate exclusively with each other unless or until one of them dies. The project continually updates a coyote family tree from its two decades of DNA collection.

Back at the green space, Shane continues to peer into hollow logs and double-check rock piles for pups. No luck. Did coyote 1035 and her mate move the pups completely out of the green space? The constant roar of traffic makes that seem impossible. Could they carry pups one by one across busy roads and intersections? Shane thinks it's possible. "The mom was born on a golf course nearby," he says. She knows how to cross highways.

"I don't want to give up," Shane says while searching. To him, coyote 1035 isn't just a tracking frequency on the VHF receiver. She's a living, breathing coyote Shane's known for years. Of course he wants to find her pups. "That's what makes this project so unique," says Shane. "We know the individual." Finding this coyote will have to wait for another day, however. Other dens await discovery.

HIKE, BIKE, PUP

Irritated cyclists and joggers shoot dirty looks at the pickup trucks creeping along the hike-and-bike trail. Who can blame them? A traffic jam of bikes, walkers, strollers, leashed dogs, and sweaty runners clog the popular seven-mile (11.3-kilometer) paved loop. Luckily, the den-searching group doesn't have far to drive. Searchers soon park the vehicles off the trail, and the endless parade of urban exercisers resumes.

Everyone at the Urban Coyote Research Project looks forward to pupping season. Every year, county naturalists, ecologists, and wildlife workers join the search, hoping to see coyote pups in the wild. This morning's team members tumble out of the trucks, slap on sunscreen and bug spray, cross the paved trail, and fan out into the forest.

Most wear long sleeves and pants even though the temperature will hit ninety degrees Fahrenheit (thirty-two Celsius) to protect themselves from fresh leaves of poison ivy glistening with itch-inducing oil, mosquitoes buzzing with hunger, and ticks crawling everywhere, not to mention thorns and briars. While not a place for bare skin, it is the last recorded tracking location of a denning collared coyote. These marshy woods shelter her pups somewhere.

Coyote parents put a lot of work into hiding their dens. The intrepid searchers spend the next couple of hours tramping painstakingly back and forth through thick swampy brush. They examine every hole and shine flashlights into one hollow tree after another. Dripping with sweat and splattered in mud, the den seekers get down on their hands and knees to look for nearly invisible bits of fuzzy fur or try to catch a whiff of unbathed-dog scent. (Eww.)

Someone points out paw tracks in mud. "Dog," says Shane. "Too big for coyotes." A trail hiker shuffling by with music blaring doesn't stop to ask what the sweaty searchers are seeking. After an hour fighting off bugs and wandering in the heat, what doesn't look like a possible den site? What about that dead tree? Did someone search that pile of rocks? It's easy to end up walking in circles, though it's impossible to get lost with the nearby highway noise.

Stopping to drink some water, urban-wildlife tech Blake Graber hears yelling. "Shane's found a den!" he says, and takes off running. Finally! Text messages go out and soon the whole gang gathers around a big old toppled tree.

A large split in the fallen tree's trunk leads to a dark, hollowed-out space inside the log. Strong flashlight beams reveal a squinting cuddle puddle of pups. How'd Shane know to look in there? "The fur caught my eye," he says, pointing to a couple of tiny wisps of fuzz snagged on crumbling bark. Really?

The parents chose a good den. They safely stashed the pups deep inside the narrow log. Fortunately, the brave (and thin) researcher Zach Hahn offers to squeeze himself into the hollow log's opening. Channeling his inner otter (he studies urban river otters), Zach slowly shimmies headfirst into the

Coyote pups inside a hollow log.

ZACH PASSES PUPS OUT TO BLAKE FROM DEEP INSIDE THE HOLLOW LOG.

hole. He inches up inside it until only his legs are visible. Luckily there's enough room for him to reach an arm up over his head to the pups. The fluffy youngsters go into escape mode, rolling around and trying to climb deeper into the tree and farther from the grabby blue-gloved hand. Run away!

Zach gently snags a wriggly pup, slides it down his body, and passes it out of the hole to Blake. One pup. Then he goes for another. Two pups. Then a third and fourth. "Done," says Zach. Blake grabs a shin and helps pull Zach out. "That's all there were," says Zach, brushing reddish sawdust out of his beard.

The four coyote pups are milk-chocolate brown and deliciously adorable. They are small and furry with tiny, floppy ears on humpy round heads, and they seem to have no necks, just a body that's mostly belly with short legs. They look more like miniature bear cubs than pups, down to their teeny, widely spaced claws. One of the pups barely has its eyes open. That puts these canid cuties under two weeks of age.

After a few moments of oohing and aahing, the crew members settle onto the forest floor and begin the real work. The urban-wildlife techs dig out equipment, pull out clipboards, and organize instruments. Time to microchip the four coyote pups.

Just like when the captured adult coyotes get collars, each pup has its details

◄ A coyote pup gets its exam.

▲ This coyote pup is less than two weeks old.

▼ Cara and Emily weigh a coyote pup.

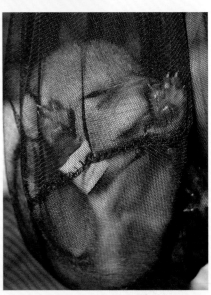

▲ Coyote pups are weighed in net bags.

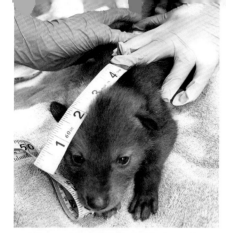

▲ Measuring a pup's body length.

▲ Next up, ear-height measuring.

▼ Microchips are implanted under the skin with a needle.

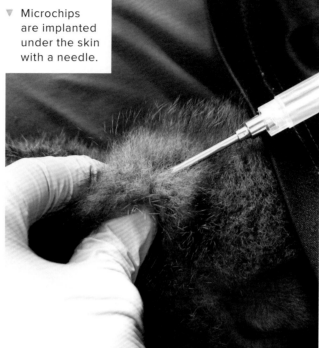

recorded—weight, length, paw measurements, teeth inspection, parasite check—its fur collected, and its blood drawn. Then a tech carefully injects a microchip, not much bigger than a cooked grain of rice, under the skin of each pup. The microchips are the same kind that veterinarians implant in pets.

All the pups get registered in the project's database. If one of them is captured in the future, a scan of the microchip will give researchers a number that will lead to all its information, including where it was born.

Meanwhile, Shane takes another look around. Four is a low litter number for coyotes. Parents sometimes split up litters, stashing some pups in a second den, so Shane grabs his flashlight and goes searching.

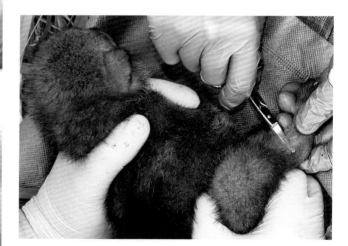

▲ Fur samples are collected from each pup.

◄ Teeth get checked too.

55

Coyote Capture Form

Coyote ID #:

Study Area: Por...

Trap Location

Easting   Northing:

Capture Method:

Drug: Lot #:   Dosage 1:

Sex: ♂   Age (if Known):

Total Length   in. Tail Length:

Right Hind Foot Length:

Physical Condition: *Poor / Good / Excellent*

Reproductive Condition:

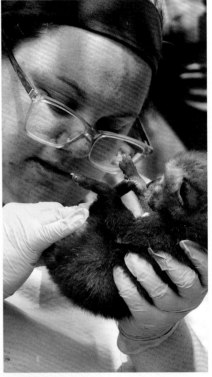

RESEARCHERS NOTE DOWN
ALL THE INFORMATION ON THE
SAME FORMS THEY USE FOR
THE ADULT CAPTURED COYOTES.

▲ Learning to tell males from females takes practice.

◀ Researchers double-check the microchip number on the red chip reader.

SUPERCHARGED REPRODUCERS

A million years of evolution has fashioned an incredible reproduction system in coyotes, one that's helped them dodge extermination.

First is pack life. Living in family groups boosts coyote litter numbers. Male coyotes deliver food to the mother and pups, protect them from predators, and shuttle pups between dens if needed. It takes a pack to raise pups. Though most coyotes usually have six or so pups, they can have thirteen to fourteen, explains Stan. By comparison, six kittens is a big litter for a bobcat, a mammal about the same size as a coyote. But bobcat moms don't have help. These furry single moms raise kittens alone.

If a pregnant coyote is underfed or unhealthy, her body will absorb some of the microscopic pup embryos. "She'll only have a litter of three or four pups, even though there were ten [embryos]," explains Stan. This happens with bobcats too—lean years cause smaller litters.

But even when food and other resources are plentiful, bobcat litters still max out around six. A healthy coyote mother with plenty to eat can give birth to twice that many pups. "Their mating system allows them to increase their reproductive capacity," explains Stan. And quickly.

Big litters are just one element of coyote-mating-system success. Unlike human teens, young coyotes' time to maturity can speed up too. Spoiled youngsters growing up with little competition for food, space, and territories breed sooner and younger.

▶ Exhausted pups get back to the business of snuggling and sleeping.

▲ Blake returns the pups to their den, no worse for wear.

"That goes back to their social system," says Stan. "Coyotes are territorial animals with a really strong monogamous [one-mate] system." Having territories to defend and living in packs has given them a kind of coyote radar. They're hyperaware of other coyotes around them and know *how many* live nearby. In other words, coyotes sense their own population density.

Carrying capacity is the term for how many animals a place can support (not how many snacks fit in a backpack). "Coyotes don't really exceed their carrying capacity," says Stan. Instead of over-populating and then starving, coyotes simply fill up whatever the landscape can hold—and no more.

Coyotes don't decide to reproduce less. Pregnant females can't choose a litter size. Nor do pups debate when to find mates and start breeding. These responses happen automatically, thanks to coyote hormones. Chemical signals likely carry and convey the messages.

All dogs, wild and domestic, do a lot of sniff-ing. Scents are chemical compounds that canids get a lot of information from. (Yes, that blade of grass *is* that interesting.) A coyote continually marks its own territory by peeing and pooping around the area. It also constantly smells and decodes whatever scents—or other chemical mes-sages and signals—it encounters.

▶ Like all canids, coyotes sense the world through smell.

The chemical signals a coyote receives can set off hormones. "And then that creates the reproductive response," explains Stan. For example, a female who comes across lots of stinky stranger-coyote scents will have a smaller litter than one who doesn't encounter those coyote-overcrowding messages. Pretty neat, huh?

Pups who grow up with too many coyote neighbors also stay with their parents longer. They put off seeking mates and starting packs of their own. "*How many neighbors do we have, how many packs are living near us?* Those young animals are getting those signals too," says Stan. "Coyotes communicate across packs in other ways as well." Every furry triangular ear tunes in when nearby packs yip and howl. Messages can be seen, smelled, or heard.

"One of the things that's a big mystery for us researchers is pack size," says Stan. A coyote pack can be an alpha pair plus one or a group of four or five grown offspring living with parents. Why do some offspring leave and some stay? Messages of some sort influence the decisions, says Stan. Whether its hormone-triggering scents, nerve-firing sounds, or something else isn't completely clear yet. "There's a lot of different layers to the life of the coyote." Very fascinating layers.

CHAPTER SIX
COYOTE COEXISTENCE

Emily Zepeda has studied the behavior of all sorts of creatures, from bioluminescent squid to bumblebees. But nothing compares to coyotes.

"They're so interesting," says Emily. "And they do all kinds of crazy things." The time she's spent studying coyotes in their adopted urban habitat has only bolstered her respect for them. "You sometimes are wondering why, and *how*, they do all these amazing feats."

Emily holds up the antenna and listens for the beeping signal of a collared coyote. She's doing more than simply tracking the animal. Emily uses the changing sound of the beeps to estimate when the coyote runs away, and later she'll calculate how far it went. This is called the flight-initiation distance, or FID.

FID measures a wild animal's tolerance of people. Think of two squirrels snacking at a

◄ Emily listens for the beeping signal of a collared coyote.

treatment period," says Emily. For a week, she located the control-group coyotes, walked in on them, and followed each for three minutes. "And for the animals in the hazing treatment, we walk in on them and haze them for three minutes." Haze how? Mostly yelling at the coyotes while following them. Once that was done, Emily went back and remeasured FIDs to see if hazing had changed their behavior.

Did hazing increase coyote FID, making them bolt from farther distances when people appeared? Unfortunately, the collected data wasn't clear one way or the other. The distances were too small to measure accurately with the technology. Plus, hazing tricky coyotes is tough. Being able to locate, haze, and then relocate a particular collared coyote multiple times wasn't easy.

"Coyotes are hard," says Stan. "I mean really, really hard." Even with fancy location-beeping technology, getting close enough to coyotes to do the hazing tests was extremely difficult. "Their senses are better than our technology," admits Stan. The coyotes often split the scene as soon as researchers showed up in their trucks. "They would know that we're coming for them."

CITY-DWELLING COYOTES MUST LEARN TO SAFELY NAVIGATE STREETS AND OTHER HUMAN-MADE BARRIERS TO FIND FOOD AND TERRITORIES.

COEXISTENCE
RESISTANCE IS FUTILE

Why put so much effort into figuring out if coyote hazing works? Cities, park departments, and the public need practical, proven methods for dealing with coyotes. Coyotes aren't simply surviving in urban areas—they're thriving. In cities, no one hunts or traps them, small prey is plentiful, and open territories are available. "Coyotes in urban areas have a better life in some ways" than country coyotes, says Shane.

Humans created a perfect coyote world: a deforested continent devoid of big predators (especially wolves) and overrun by rodents. And for once, a wild animal ended up winning. "That's part of the good news," says Stan. Coyotes don't need human help—fortunately for them. "Because if they did, we probably wouldn't help them out too much."

Neighborhoods that try to eliminate coyotes mostly fail. Transient coyotes immediately (and happily) fill any newly empty spaces. And increased litter sizes

◄ Cars, trucks, and other vehicles kill many urban coyotes, including ones collared by the project.

and earlier breeding ages quickly bump the population back up. And there's the controversy and difficult logistics of killing doglike animals in urban areas. Chicago and many other cities prohibit the firing of weapons. Snares and traps set for coyotes can accidently capture other animals (raccoons, stray dogs, skunks) and create hazards for kids and pets. Few animal control agencies have enough staffers to answer every coyote-complaint call. And hiring professionals to lethally remove (kill) "problem coyotes" gets expensive quickly.

Many people would prefer *not* to live with coyotes, but the only *Canis* species native solely to the Americas isn't going away. "It doesn't really matter what we think about coyotes," says Stan. "If they've decided they can live there, they're going to live there." Coexistence it is.

Coyote management is part of the coexistence equation. Management means dealing with problem coyotes. And hazing could be a superimportant management method, says Emily. "It's low-cost. Anybody can do it. It can be used in a number of different scenarios." Here are some examples:

A jogger in a park sees a coyote come too close.

HAZE: Yelling and waving arms runs it off.

A coyote regularly cuts through a backyard where toddlers play.

HAZE: Spraying it with a garden hose changes the coyote's route.

A dog owner fears neighborhood coyotes.

HAZE: Shaking a can of pennies before Spot goes out to potty scares coyotes away.

◀ Retired park worker John Klein educates the public about coyotes in Cincinnati, Ohio.

Studies from the Urban Coyote Research Project show that coyotes and people coexist conflict-free for the most part. Not that many people even realize coyotes live among them. (Now, *that's* conflict-free!) Stan helped many North American cities deal with booming coyote populations back in the early 2000s. "My research is to help people as well as to help wildlife," he says.

A big part of coyote and human coexistence is information and communication. Programs for schools, parks, and communities can educate the public about what coyotes do and don't do and when to worry. That knowledge helps both the two- *and* four-legged residents.

Towns and cities can also create laws that prevent people from feeding coyotes, enforce rules about keeping dogs leashed, and set up systems for reporting coyote problems. No coyote is born a troublemaker. The humans-equal-food connection turns coyotes into troublemakers.

Like most wild animals, coyotes naturally avoid people. "But you can change that if you provide food for them," says Stan. Dumping bags of dog chow in the park (yes, people do that) creates the troublesome link between humans and food for coyotes. But so does leaving pet food outside and not cleaning up spilled birdseed. Hungry, omnivorous coyotes will seek out meat and bones in compost piles, dropped fruit under trees or bushes, and fast-food trash in open bins. This kind of accidental feeding also causes coyotes to link scary humans with yummy food. And food usually wins.

COYOTE THREAT LEVEL

WHEN A COYOTE DOES THIS...	PEOPLE CAN HELP LIMIT PROBLEMS THIS WAY
• Rarely or only occasionally seen.	• Don't leave pet food outdoors. • Secure garbage containers. • Supervise pets while outside.
• Occasionally seen during the day or frequently seen at night. • Free-ranging pets disappear.	• Limit wildlife feeding. • Haze coyote with shouting and clapping and by throwing objects until chased away.
• Frequently seen during the day. • Stalking pets. • Fleeing from people.	• Continue hazing. • Stop feeding wildlife. • Investigate problem-coyote reporting locally.
• Approaching people aggressively. • Growling, barking when hazed; not intimidated or running away. • Following children. • Preying on pets in yards.	• Continue hazing. • Contact local authorities and report a problem coyote. • Stop feeding all wildlife, including birds.

CONCERN LEVEL

LOW ↓ HIGH

◄ Coyotes help control the Canada geese population by preying on their eggs.

But living with urban coyotes comes with more than challenges. The benefits are vast, not just for humans but for entire ecosystems. Coyotes could help take the greening of cities and suburbs to the next level.

The latest U.S. census found that more than 80 percent of people live in urban areas. As more people moved into cities and suburbs, they demanded more parks, more green spaces, and more enjoyable outdoor spaces. Urban wildlife has eagerly expanded into these citified habitats, flourishing in neighborhoods and preserves. Deer give birth to fawns in flower beds, geese herd goslings across city streets, and trash pandas (raccoons) earn that nickname.

But while urban ecosystems look natural, most lack big predators. Mountain lions and wolves remain unwelcome, even though deer overpopulate and have no predators in most places. Because of car collisions, deer kill more North Americans than any other wild animal. "That animal is actually a much greater risk to people than coyotes," says Stan.

Coyotes fill a predator role. They're not big enough to kill adult deer, but coyotes kill enough fawns to bring down the deer population. The project found that coyotes kill 20 to 80 percent of fawns in some Chicago locations. Not everyone likes the idea of coyotes eating cute, helpless fawns. "But," Stan says, "that's actually how nature is supposed to work." And that adorable fawn will soon be a garden-wrecking road hazard.

Another overpopulated urban animal that coyotes help control? Canada geese. The birds take over ponds, and each one drops up to two pounds of mushy poop on sidewalks and lawns per day. Coyotes prey on goose nests, eating their eggs. "That's very beneficial to us as humans," says Shane. By placing cameras near nests, the project videotaped goose-egg snatchers. "Coyotes were the number one predator."

Predators strengthen all ecosystems. By doing what predators naturally do, they improve urban environments too.

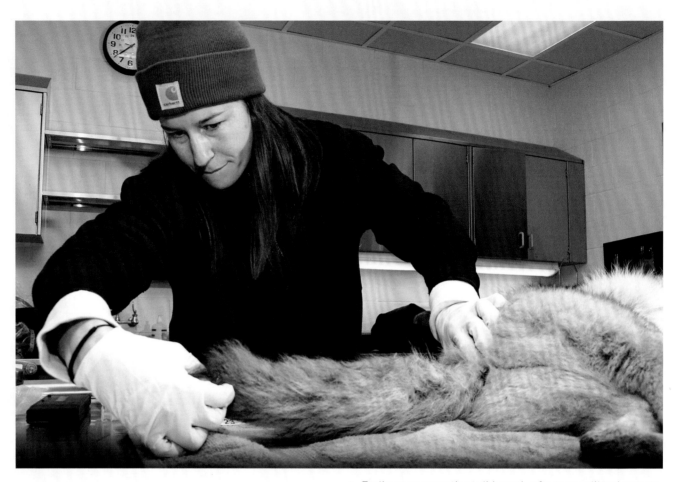

▲ Emily measures the tail length of a tranquilized coyote.

We know healthy ecosystems benefit people. After all, trees improve cities by cooling temperatures, soaking up runoff, and cleaning the air. Likewise, predators keep prey populations in check, allowing a greater variety of species to thrive. Predators boost biodiversity.

That's true for coyotes too. By eating rats and mice, they free up space and food for more species of native rodents.

EMILY TRIES TO TRACK DOWN A COLLARED COYOTE.

Another coyote-powered biodiversity bump! Why settle for mowed and manicured urban green space when cities and suburbs can host full-fledged biodiverse ecosystems? Coyotes can help make that happen.

Urban coyotes could also help update the big-bad-wolf image of predators and build appreciation for how nature works. Living separate from nature causes people to ignore it. Out of sight, out of mind, right? Jogging by a rabbit half eaten by a coyote reminds urbanites about predators and prey and other natural processes. Coyotes are teaching humans how other species live and what they need to survive. "Coyotes are basically educating people," says Stan.

What other deep knowledge or ecosystem service will this wily predator gift to humans next? "It's an evolving story," says Stan. "We don't know what the final chapter of the urban-coyote story is going to be." Only by coexisting do we get to find out.

Emily snips a sample whisker from a tranquilized coyote.

Meet a
BEHAVIORAL ECOLOGIST

Emily Zepeda grew up a city kid in San Francisco, California. She finds urban wildlife especially interesting. Coyotes moved into California's metropolitan areas decades ago. Long before working with the Urban Coyote Research Project, Emily learned about city coyotes living in San Francisco. "My dog, Steve, got into a little scuffle with a coyote at one point," she says. (Neither Steve nor the coyote was harmed.)

A college summer spent in a biochemistry lab sparked Emily's interest in science. "I really fell in love with the research process," she says. Especially all the fun problem-solving. Emily went on to study animal behavior with support from a program that guides underrepresented students into high-level science.

Becoming a scientist requires deep dives into subjects. For some, going deep leads to zeroing in. The smallest parts that make up a life-form—cells, DNA—hold answers for them. Others, like Emily, find questions that need a bigger picture to get answers.

▼ Hearing the yip or howl of a coyote reminds people that wildlife lives here too.

Emily compared how comfortable coyotes felt around people in Chicago's downtown, in the suburbs, and in forest preserves. And she explored how coyote behavior in different urban settings looped back to the reactions of those people and how they behaved toward coyotes. Her research includes the "race, wealth, and education of the humans in the landscape." Do coyotes live longer in the suburbs, where big backyards and parks provide shelter and prey? Or do vacant lots and train tracks offer safer human-free hideouts and hunting grounds?

How and where humans live affect all wildlife, not just coyotes. People reshape landscapes with roads, cities, farms, and factories. Emily's research aims to include those effects in a precise way. After all, climate change proved that ecosystems untouched by *Homo sapiens* no longer exist. Do wild animals like coyotes belong in cities? Emily thinks so. "Wildlife are as much a part of the environment as plants or the climate," she says. "I think instead of trying to resist them, we should try and work on coexisting and incorporating them into human life."

INDEX

Note: Page references in **bold** indicate photographs.

SCIENTISTS IN THE FIELD

WHERE SCIENCE MEETS ADVENTURE

Check out these titles to meet more scientists who are out in the field—and contributing every day to our knowledge of the world around us:

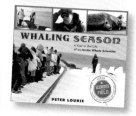

Looking for even more adventure? Craving updates on the work of your favorite scientists, as well as in-depth video footage, audio, photography, and more? Then visit the Scientists in the Field website!

www.sciencemeetsadventure.com